For everyone on Earth, especially the children,
especially those I met in Rwanda, India, Bhutan,
the Democratic Republic of Congo, Australia,
and the USA, and especially Ms. Greta's
second grade class at the Brooklyn New School.
I promised I would try to make a book about
all of us and the planet we share. This is it.

And for the real Quinn and his family,
Elliott, Caroline, and Jolyon.
You make the world a better place.

Enormous thanks to the early readers of this book, including Dhonielle Clayton.
Lisa Rose and Sumaya Teli, for their thoughtful comments and helpful insights.

Copyright © 2020 by Sophie Blackall.

Library of Congress Cataloging-in-Publication Data available.
ISBN 978-1-4521-3779-7
Manufactured in China.

Design by Sara Gillingham Studio. Typeset in Halewyn and hand lettered by Sophie Blackall.
The illustrations in this book were rendered in chinese ink and watercolor.

10 9 8 7 6 5 4

Chronicle Books LLC, 680 Second Street, San Francisco, California 94107
www.chroniclekids.com

If You Come to Earth

by Sophie Blackall

chronicle books·san francisco

Dear Visitor from Outer Space,

If you come to Earth,

here's what you need to know.

You can find us near a big sun

and a tiny moon

and a bunch of other planets.
Ours is the greeny-blue one.

The green and brown bits are land,

and the blue stuff is water.

People mostly live on the land
in big cities

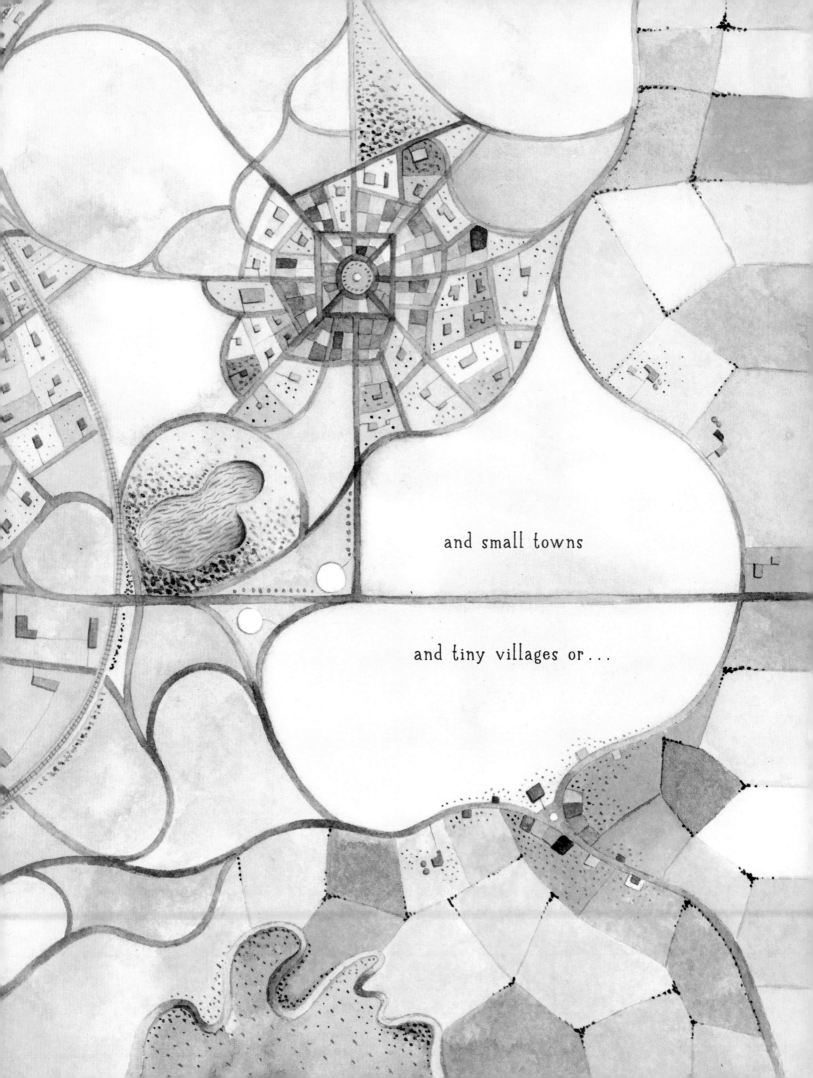

and small towns

and tiny villages or...

just in the middle of nowhere.

We live in all kinds of homes.

In all kinds of families.

There are more than seven billion people on Earth.

We all have bodies.

But every body is different.

Except for my friends who are identical twins
and look the same.

Except for Mustafa's mole.

Inside our heads, we are usually thinking.

You can't see our thoughts,

but sometimes we show our feelings on our faces.

Even if we don't feel like it,
we get dressed every day.

We wear different clothes,
depending on what we do

and where we live
and if it's hot or cold.

There's lots of different weather in the world.

Some of it's good and some of it's bad.

Wherever people live, we usually have to go someplace else.

There are lots of ways to get there.

I'm a kid and kids go to school
to learn stuff,
so we'll know what to do
when we're grown up.

Grown-ups do lots of things

to make the world work.

But when people are not at work or at school or sick or asleep,

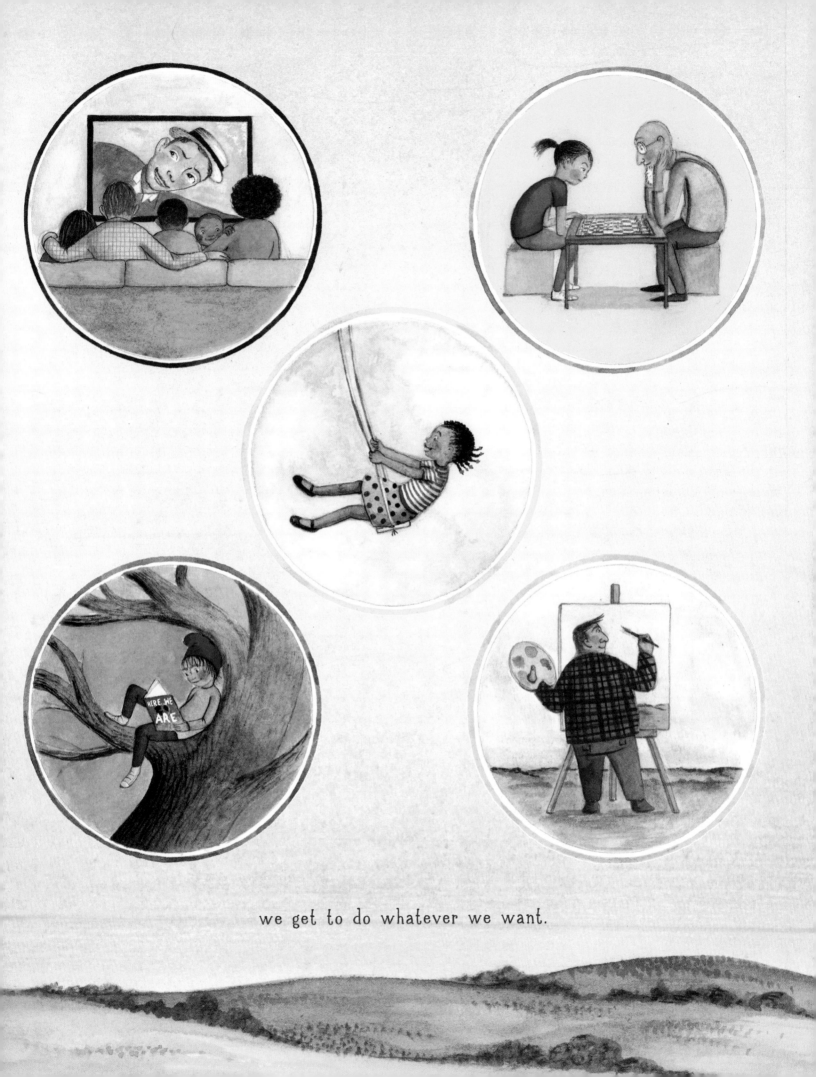

we get to do whatever we want.

Whatever we are doing, we need to eat when we are hungry.

Some of us have more food than others.

We all need food and water to survive.

We get water from the rain,

which flows into little streams

and big rivers

and all the way to the sea.

You can't drink the sea
because it's too salty.

The sea looks empty . . .

but actually, it's full.

Fish can swim, but they can't walk.

Most animals can walk or swim or gallop or hop,

but they can't fly.

I can fly!

Some birds can swim and walk and fly,

so if I had to choose, I'd be a bird.

Birds can sing,

so can whales

and people.

People make all kinds of music,

on our own

and all together.

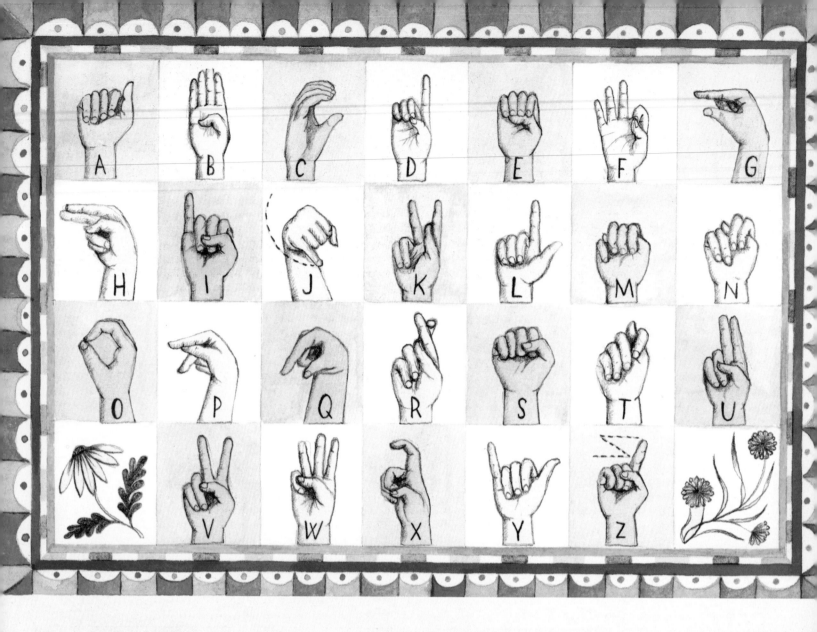

Some of us who are deaf talk with our hands and faces.

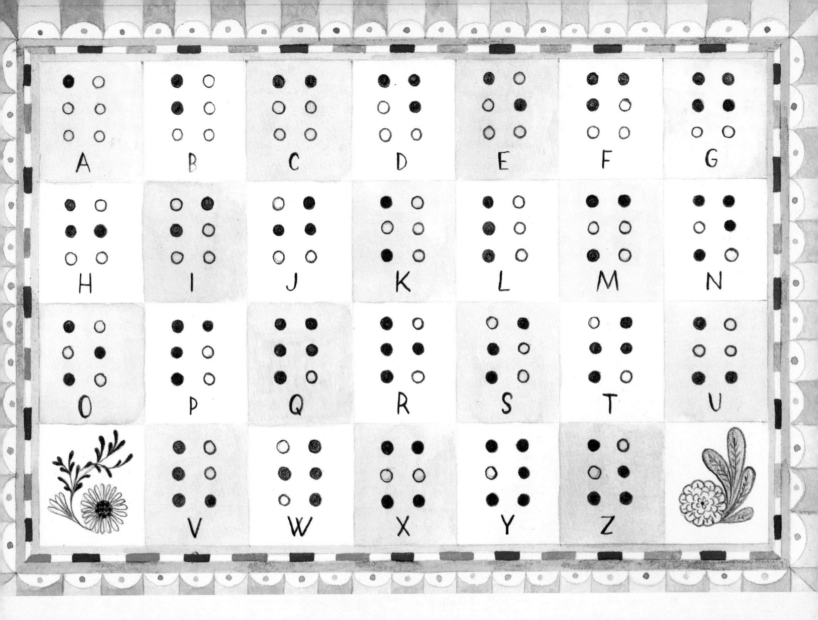

Some of us who are blind read with our fingers.

If we are blind, we can imagine colors
as shapes and sounds.

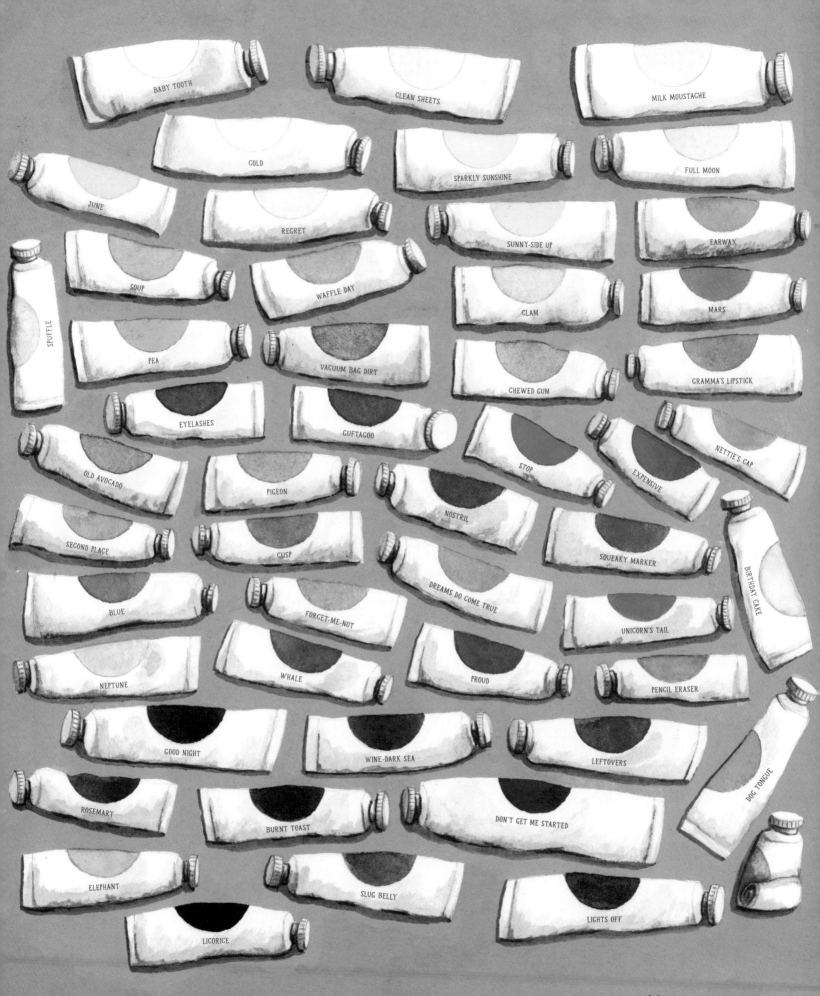

These are the colors you need to paint everything in the world.

Some things are part of nature.

Some things are made by people.

Some things are big.

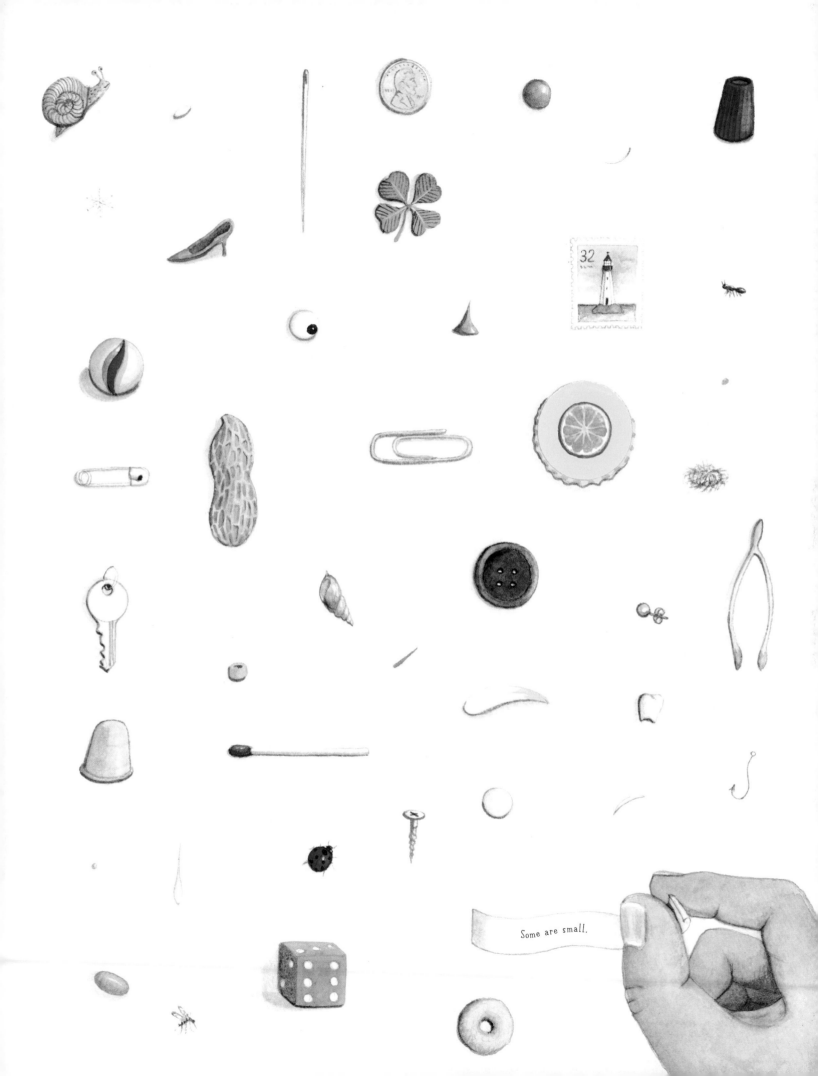

Some are small.

Some things are invisible.

wind

invisible cloak

ghosts

gravity

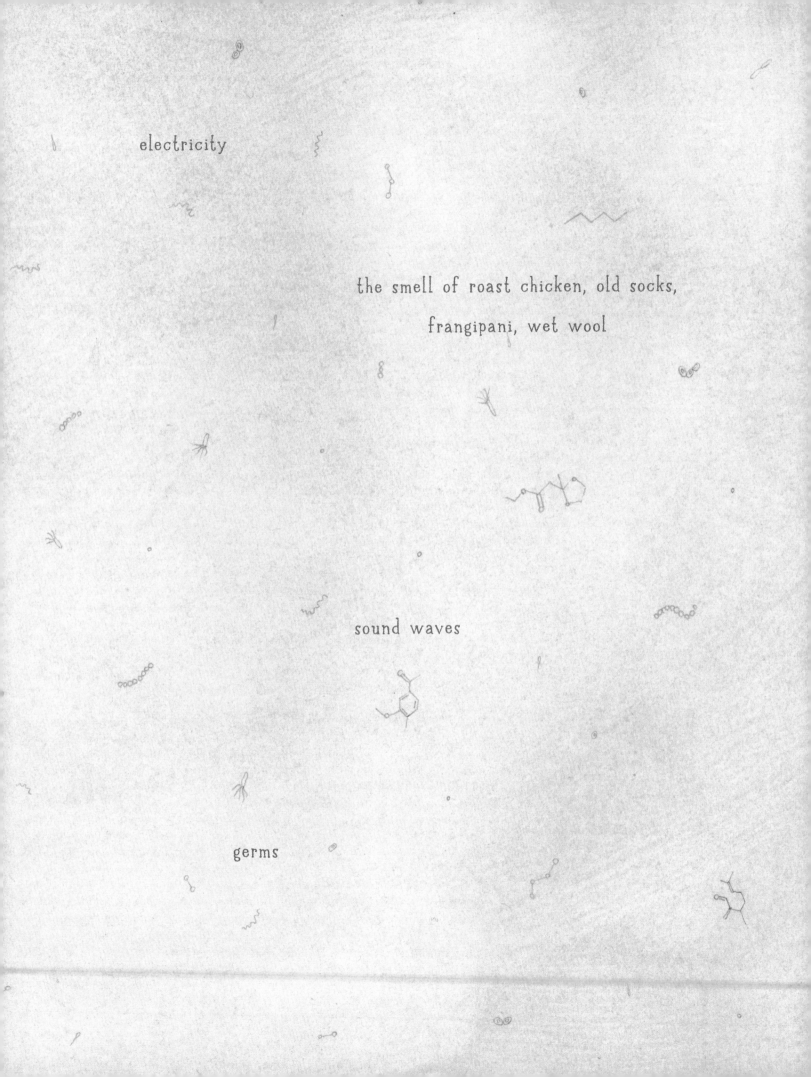

electricity

the smell of roast chicken, old socks,
frangipani, wet wool

sound waves

germs

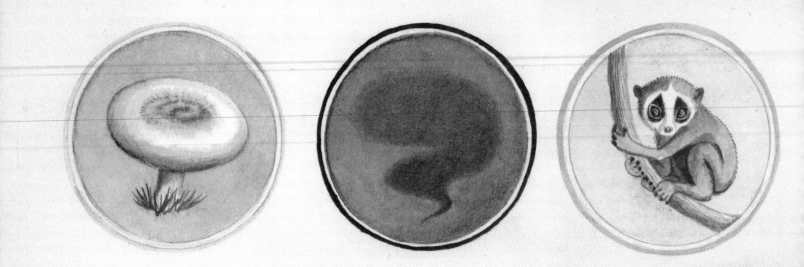

Some germs can make you sick.

So can eating a woolly milkcap toadstool

or breathing in smoke or getting spat on by a slow loris.

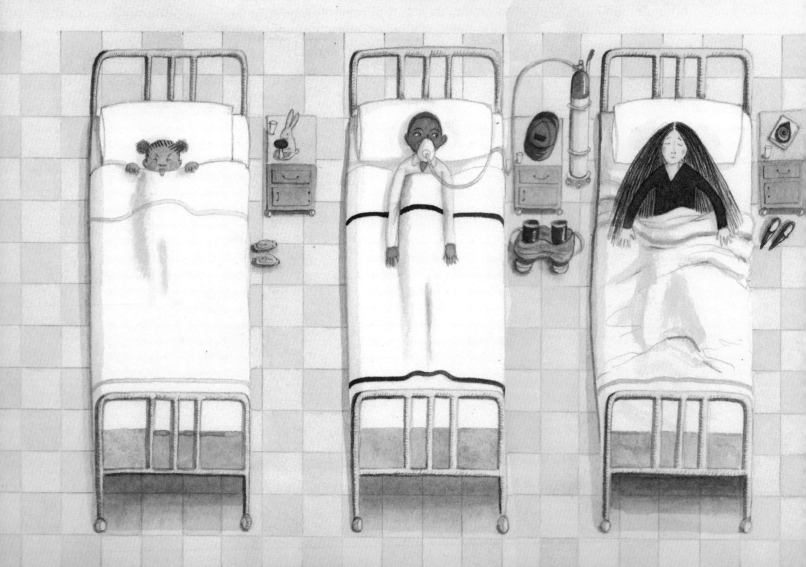

Sometimes people get hurt by accident.

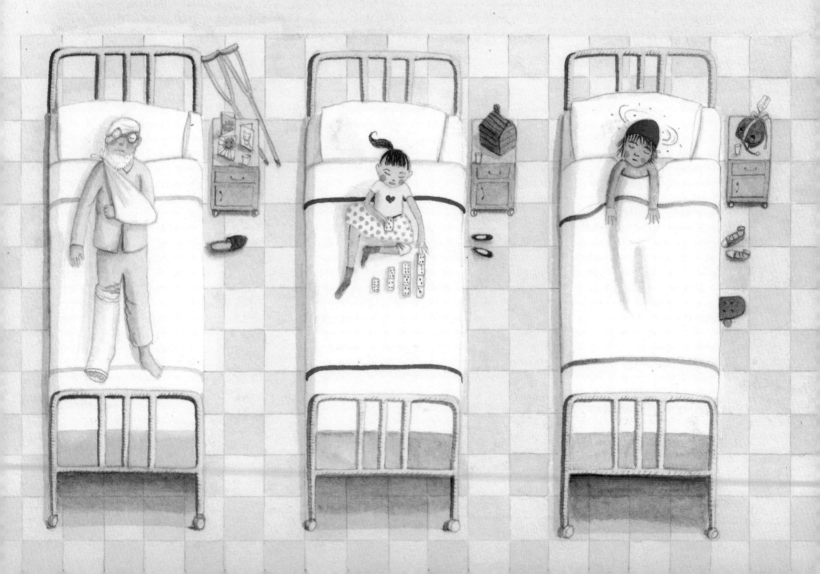

we hurt each other.

It's better when we help each other.

Kids are good at
lots of things.

Babies are
not very good at
anything.

Grown-ups can do
just about anything until
they are really, *really* old.

But by then,
the babies are grown up
and can help.

Older people are good at telling stories about the world when they were young.

Kids are good at
making up stories that
haven't happened yet.

There are lots of things we don't know.
We don't know where we were before we were born
or where we go when we die.

But right this minute,
we are here together on this beautiful planet.

If you come to Earth, you can stay in my room.

P.S.

How many eyes do you have?

Are you small or big?

Do you have any pets?

When is your birthday?

Is it always dark where you are?

Are you going to visit us?

———

My friends and I want to know.

The idea for this book arrived on top of a Himalayan mountain in Bhutan.

I was working with Save the Children and had climbed a zigzagging path to reach

a tiny two-room school with ten students.

We couldn't understand a word each other said,

but the children drew pictures for me and shared their lunch,

and I showed them some books. I have made books about boars and babies and bears and lighthouses,

but what I wanted in that moment was a book that would bring us together. A book about their home and mine.

I wished for the same book when I was with children in Rwanda and the Democratic Republic of the Congo, in India and

Singapore, and in Brooklyn, New York. And so, I decided I would make such a book. But I was going to need lots of help.

I talked to children all over the world and spent time at the Brooklyn New School where I made 23 new

friends who gave me lots of ideas about how to explain our world to someone from outer space. Those children,

Ava, Alex, Ari, Athena, Bernadette, Callum, Carolina, Denbele, Earon, Finn, Goriola, Gus, Ida, Iris, Karen, Lucia,

Markell, Mia, Moxie, Nile, Noon, Tehutiamenra, and Willa are the students in the classroom image in this book,

along with their teacher, Ms. Greta. I am grateful to them for their thoughtful, hilarious ideas. I told them making

a book takes a while. I didn't expect it to take five years.

As the idea for the book took shape, I knew there needed to be one kid writing the letter. I'd met thousands

of smart, endearing children—how could I possibly choose only one to be our narrator? Then I met Quinn.

Quinn has lived in Nigeria and Indonesia and Nepal, but when we met, he and his family were living in Australia.

Quinn's brother, Elliott, was busy with a lizard, so I asked Quinn all the questions, ending with, "What kind of snack

would you give a visitor from another planet?"

"Mashed potatoes," he said without hesitation. "Because we don't know if they have teeth." And then he slid

over 17 drawings he'd made on flash cards while we were talking, of different planets and their possible inhabitants.

I had my kid.

There are nearly eight billion people on Earth. I could only fit a small number into this book. Some are

my friends and neighbors; some are families I saw picnicking in Central Park. Some I met at a market in Yangon,

on a bus in Beijing, on a boat in Sydney, in a cow stall on a dairy farm in Hobart, New York. Almost everyone in

this book is based on a real person. Some of them, like a few in the pages about things grown-ups do, are people

you might recognize.

We humans define ourselves by where we were born, where we live, what we believe, by the clothes we wear,

and the languages we speak. But there is no "typical" person. We are all different.

Yet there's something we all share—the planet on which we live. This world of ice-capped mountains

and sandy deserts and grassy plains, of winding rivers and glacial lakes and glittering seas, of bustling cities and busy

towns and sleepy villages. This world that contains all our food and all our water and all the art and books and

music, and every ant and every sneeze and every comma, every atom of every living, and nonliving, thing.

This planet that carries all that we hold dear orbits the sun in our solar system. The sun is a star,

and it's one of billions of stars in our galaxy, which we call the Milky Way. The Milky Way is one of billions

of galaxies in the known universe. Astronomers estimate there may be billions of other planets a bit like

Earth where life-forms could exist.

There are lots of things I don't know. I don't know if there is life elsewhere in the universe, though

I find it hard to believe we are all alone. But I do know this: Right this minute, we are all here together

on this beautiful planet. It's the only one we have, so we should take care of it.

And each other. Don't you think?

Sophie Blackall